MAR 1 3 2006

P9-CFS-504

A Note to Parents and Caregivers:

Read-it! Readers are for children who are just starting on the amazing road to reading. These beautiful books support both the acquisition of reading skills and the love of books.

The RED LEVEL presents familiar topics using common words and repeating sentence patterns.

The BLUE LEVEL presents new ideas using a larger vocabulary and varied sentence structure.

The YELLOW LEVEL presents more challenging ideas, a broad vocabulary, and wide variety in sentence structure.

The GREEN LEVEL presents more complex ideas, an extended vocabulary range, and expanded language structures.

When sharing a book with your child, read in short stretches, pausing often to talk about the pictures. Have your child turn the pages and point to the pictures and familiar words. And be sure to reread favorite stories or parts of stories.

There is no right or wrong way to share books with children. Find time to read with your child, and pass on the legacy of literacy.

Adria F. Klein, Ph.D.
Professor Emeritus
California State University
San Bernardino, California

Managing Editor: Bob Temple
Creative Director: Terri Foley
Editor: Brenda Haugen
Editorial Adviser: Andrea Cascardi
Copy Editor: Laurie Kahn
Designer: Melissa Voda
Page production: The Design Lab
The illustrations in this book were prepared digitally.

Picture Window Books
5115 Excelsior Boulevard
Suite 232
Minneapolis, MN 55416
1-877-845-8392
www.picturewindowbooks.com

Printed in the United States of America.

Library of Congress Cataloging-in-Publication Data
Blair, Eric.
The boy who cried wolf : a retelling of Aesop's fable / by Eric Blair ; illustrated by Dianne
Silverman.
p. cm. — (Read-it! readers)
Summary: A retelling of the fable in which a young boy's false cries for help cause him
problems when he is really in need of assistance.
ISBN 1-4048-0319-X (Reinforced Library Binding)
[1. Fables. 2. Folklore.] I. Aesop. II. Silverman, Dianne, ill. III.
Title. IV. Series.
PZ8.2.B595 Bo 2004
398.2—dc22

2003016677

The Boy Who Cried Wolf

A Retelling of Aesop's Fable
By Eric Blair

Illustrated by Dianne Silverman

Content Adviser:
Kathy Baxter, M.A.
Former Coordinator of Children's Services
Anoka County (Minnesota) Library

Reading Advisers:
Adria F. Klein, Ph.D.
Professor Emeritus, California State University
San Bernardino, California

Susan Kesselring, M.A.
Literacy Educator
Rosemount-Apple Valley-Eagan (Minnesota) School Dist

Picture Window Books
Minneapolis, Minnesota

What Is a Fable?

A fable is a story that teaches a lesson.
In some fables, animals may talk and act
the way people do. A Greek slave named
Aesop created some of the world's favorite
fables. Aesop's fables have been enjoyed
by readers for more than 2,000 years.

Once upon a time, there was a young shepherd boy.

Every morning, the boy took his father's sheep to graze on a mountain pasture outside the village.

All day he stayed in the lonely
pasture with the sheep.

One day, the boy was bored.
He decided to play a joke
on the villagers.

He ran to the village and cried,
"Wolf! Help! There is a wolf attacking
my sheep!"

The kind villagers left their work and came running to chase the wolf away.

11

But it was a trick.

The sheep were grazing peacefully.
There was no wolf.

13

14

The boy laughed. How easily
he had fooled them!

The boy played the same trick
again and again.

Each time the villagers came running.
Each time there was no wolf.

One day, wolves really did attack
the boy's sheep.

The frightened boy ran to the village
and screamed, "Help! Wolves are
attacking my sheep!"

But no one listened to the boy.
No one came to help.

The villagers didn't believe the boy,
and the wolves ate his sheep.

Because the boy had lied so many times,
nobody believed him, even when
he was telling the truth.

23

Levels for *Read-it!* Readers

Read-it! Readers help children practice early reading skills
with brightly illustrated stories.

Red Level: Familiar topics with frequently used words and
repeating patterns.

Blue Level: New ideas with a larger vocabulary and a variety
of language structures.

The Donkey in the Lion's Skin, by Eric Blair 1-4048-0320-3

The Goose that Laid the Golden Egg, by Mark White 1-4048-0219-3

Yellow Level: Challenging ideas with an expanded vocabulary
and a wide variety of sentences.

The Ant and the Grasshopper, by Mark White 1-4048-0217-7

The Boy Who Cried Wolf, by Eric Blair 1-4048-0319-X

The Country Mouse and the City Mouse, by Eric Blair 1-4048-0318-1

The Crow and the Pitcher, by Eric Blair 1-4048-0322-X

The Dog and the Wolf, by Eric Blair 1-4048-0323-8

The Fox and the Grapes, by Mark White 1-4048-0218-5

The Tortoise and the Hare, by Mark White 1-4048-0215-0

The Wolf in Sheep's Clothing, by Mark White 1-4048-0220-7

Green Level: More complex ideas with an extended vocabulary
range and expanded language structures.

Belling the Cat, by Eric Blair 1-4048-0321-1

The Lion and the Mouse, by Mark White 1-4048-0216-9